MW01118409

Inside the NFL

THE
DENVER
BRONCOS

BOB ITALIA
ABDO & Daughters

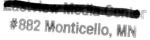

Published by Abdo & Daughters, 4940 Viking Drive, Suite 622, Edina, Minnesota 55435.

Copyright © 1996 by Abdo Consulting Group, Inc., Pentagon Tower, P.O. Box 36036, Minneapolis, Minnesota 55435 USA. International copyrights reserved in all countries. No part of this book may be reproduced in any form without written permission from the publisher.

Printed in the United States.

Cover Photo credit: Wide World Photos/Allsport
Interior Photo credits: Allsport, page 17
                    Wide World Photos, pages 4-6, 8-16, 18-21, 23, 25, 26

Edited by Kal Gronvall

Library of Congress cataloging-in-Publication Data

Italia, Bob, 1955—
      The Denver Broncos / Bob Italia
      p.   cm. — (Inside the NFL)
      Includes index.
      Summary: Traces the history of the Denver Broncos from their entry into professional football in 1960, up through their super bowl games.
      ISBN 1-56239-459-2
      1. Denver Broncos (football team)—juvenile literature. [1. Denver Broncos (football team) 2. football—History.] I. Title. II. Series: Italia, Bob, 1955— Inside the NFL.
      GV956.D37I83   1995
      796.332'64'0978883—dc20   95-7708
                                                                 CIP
                                                                 AC

CONTENTS

From Obscurity to Greatness

During the 1960s, the Denver Broncos were not impressive. They had a few great players like Lionel Taylor, Floyd Little, and Jim Turner. But Denver never struck fear in opponents' hearts.

All that changed in the mid-1970s. A new management acquired talented defensive players like Lyle Alzado, Tom Jackson, and Karl Mecklenburg. The "Orange Crush" was born, and terrorized opposing teams until the 1980s.

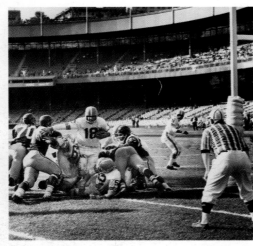

Denver Broncos quarterback Frank Tripucka plunges across the goal line in 1962.

Even after the Orange Crush disbanded, the Broncos did not disappear. In fact, their greatest years were just ahead. Quarterback John Elway would lead the charge to four Super Bowls.

Though the Broncos never won a National Football League (NFL) championship, few teams experienced Denver's success in such a short time. With Elway still at quarterback, the Broncos are poised to capture that elusive Super Bowl win.

Lionel Taylor, offensive end for the Denver Broncos, 1966.

An Ugly Team

In 1960, the Denver Broncos joined the American Football League. Named after a 1920s Denver baseball team, the Broncos had football's ugliest uniforms. Manager Dean Griffing had a small equipment budget. He bought brown jerseys and gold pants from the bankrupt Copper Bowl. Even worse were stockings with vertical brown-and-yellow stripes. The players were so upset they offered to buy their own socks. But management refused to listen.

In their first game, halfback Gene Mongo returned a punt 76 yards for a touchdown. The Broncos beat the Boston Patriots 13-10. But Denver's main offensive weapon, end Lionel Taylor, did not join the team until the season's third week of the season.

Taylor practiced with the Broncos for four days before catching 11 passes against the New York Titans. He caught enough passes in 12 games to lead the league in receiving.

The Broncos offense was built around the pass. Frank Tripucka threw 478 passes for the season, including 52 against the Houston Oilers. The Bronco defense, however, couldn't stop opponents. The Broncos lost their last eight games and finished 4-9-1.

Quarterback Frank Tripucka quarterback of the Denver Broncos.

6

No Running Game

The next season was even worse as the Denver running game finished last in the league. The passing game remained the only threat. Taylor set a professional football record with 100 catches for the season. But the Broncos lost their last seven games after a 3-4 start. Coach Frankie Filhock was fired.

In 1962, new coach Jack Faulkner decided to get new uniforms. He changed the team's colors to orange and blue. Then he announced the Great Sock Barbecue. Faulkner invited players and fans to a giant bonfire at the Broncos' practice field. The players ran laps around the field. Then they tossed their old socks into a bonfire. The new Denver Broncos had been born.

The Broncos had more success in 1962. Tripucka threw passes to Taylor, Gene Prebola, Bob Scarpitto, and Bo Dickinson. The Broncos won seven of their first nine games and contended for the Western title. But without a running attack, the Broncos lost their last five games and finished at 7-7. Still, three Broncos won individual titles: Taylor led the league in receiving, Mingo led in scoring and field goals, and Jim Fraser was the AFL's best punter.

In 1963, rookie fullback Billy Joe gave the Broncos a running game. But Tripucka's arm was getting weak, and he quit after the second game. Rookie quarterback Mickey Slaughter took over and won two games in a row, but then a knee injury ended his season. The Broncos lost their remaining games and finished 2-11-1.

Lou Saban

From 1964 to 1966, the Broncos did not play well. Management named Lou Saban as head coach and general manager. Saban immediately rebuilt the team. He traded with San Diego to get quarterback Steve Tensi, then added halfback Floyd Little with a round-one draft pick.

After losing their first three games in 1968, Denver won four in a row before losing to the San Diego Chargers. The Broncos defense was strong, anchored by All-Pro end Rich Jackson. Rookie quarterback Marlin Briscoe led the offense with his scrambling and clutch passing.

Floyd Little, running back for the Denver Broncos.

Injuries to quarterback Steve Tensi, receivers Mike Haffner and Bill Van Heusen, and Floyd Little ruined the 1969 season as the Broncos finished 5-8-1. In 1970, the Broncos stormed to a 4-1 record. But Tensi was reinjured and the Broncos lost their momentum. On the bright side, Floyd Little became an All-Pro.

In 1971, the Broncos finished with a 4-9-1 record. Tensi quit, and Saban left after nine games. With nine losing seasons behind them, it was time for a change.

John Ralston

In 1972, the Broncos hired John Ralston—their seventh head coach. Ralston had led Stanford University to two straight Rose Bowl victories. He intended to make the Broncos winners, too.

Ralston wanted a veteran quarterback to lead his young offense, so he traded for Charley Johnson of the Houston Oilers. Ralston also traded veteran defensive linemen Richard Jackson and Dave Costa. But their replacements—Lyle Alzado, Paul Smith, Pete Duranko, and Lloyd Voss—gave Denver a potent pass rush.

In 1973, Denver fought for first place all season long. Rookies Barney Chavous and Calvin Jones made a good defense even better. Veteran tackle Paul Smith became an All-Pro.

On the last day of the season, the Broncos had a showdown with the Oakland Raiders for the Western division title. Trailing 14-10 in the fourth quarter, the Broncos faked a punt on fourth down. But Bill Van Heusen could not get the first down. The Raiders scored another touchdown and the Broncos settled for

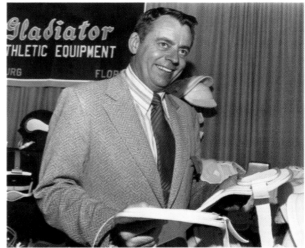

Denver coach John Ralston looks over shoulder and hip pads.

second place. Their 7-5-2 record gave them their first winning season.

In 1974, Denver fans expected the Broncos to make the playoffs. But the Broncos played inconsistently all season. Tight end Riley Odoms became an All-Pro. Second-year running back Otis Armstrong won the rushing title with 1,407 yards.

In 1975, the Broncos won their first two games, but then went into a tailspin. Armstrong was lost for the season with an injury, and Charley Johnson had trouble generating any kind of offense. At season's end, Johnson and Little retired.

The next season, Denver had its best season to date, finishing 9-5. But a loss at New England ended their playoff hopes. Still, the Broncos defense ranked second in the AFC in fewest points allowed and in rushing defense. Linebackers Tom Jackson and Randy Gradishar were the defensive standouts. Kick return specialist Rick Upchurch averaged a league-high 13.7 yards per punt return and scored four touchdowns. But failing to make the playoffs cost Ralston his job.

Denver running back Otis Armstrong busts through the Pittsburgh defensive line.

Tight end Riley Odoms breaks a tackle by the Seahawks.

The Orange Crush

Red Miller's arrival signaled a new beginning. He built a rock-solid defense that became known as the Orange Crush, and starred Lyle Alzado, Rubin Carter, Randy Gradishar, Tom Jackson, Louie Wright, and Bill Thompson.

Orange Crush defenseman, Tom Jackson, sacks Chargers quarterback Dan Fouts.

Veteran quarterback Craig Morton led the offense. Morton came to Denver in a minor trade. He led the Broncos to victory over the Raiders, Steelers, and Colts. For his efforts, Morton was named the NFL's Comeback Player of the Year.

Denver's tough defense and error-free offense took the 12-2 Broncos to the playoffs for the first time. In the playoffs, Denver won 34-21 over Pittsburgh as they broke a 21-21 tie with 13 unanswered fourth-quarter points. The defense forced four turnovers, including two interceptions by All-Pro linebacker Tom Jackson. Now they would play the Raiders for a trip to the Super Bowl.

In the AFC championship game at Denver's Mile High Stadium, the Raiders were slight favorites. They took an early 3-0 lead, but Morton struck two plays later on a 74-yard bomb to wide receiver Haven Moses.

After taking a 7-3 halftime lead, the Broncos scored in the third quarter on a Jon Keyworth touchdown run. The Raiders responded with another touchdown. But then Morton connected with Moses on a 12-yard touchdown pass. With three minutes remaining, Oakland cut the lead to three points. But the Broncos ran out the clock. They had finally reached the Super Bowl.

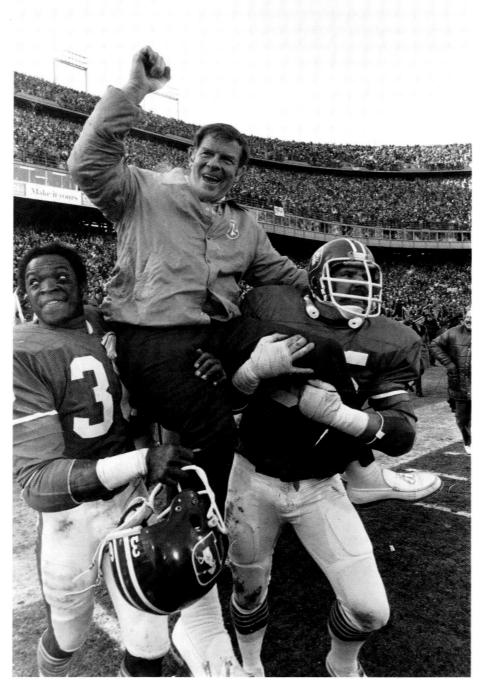

Red Miller is carried from the field after the Broncos beat the Oakland Raiders for the AFC championship.

Super Bowl Fever

In Super Bowl XII at the Super Dome in Louisiana, the Cowboys crushed Denver 27-10 in the first Super Bowl played indoors. The Dallas running game plowed through the left side of the Bronco defense. And the Cowboys defense forced Morton to throw four interceptions.

Lyle Alzado was the leader of the Orange Crush.

Having experienced Super Bowl fever, Denver started the 1978 season hoping to win it all. The Orange Crush defense played well. They allowed fewer than 13 points per game as the Broncos won the division with a 10-6 record.

But the offense struggled all season. Morton shared duties with Norris Weese and Craig Penrose. Kick returner Rick Upchurch was their most potent offensive player. In the first round of the playoffs, the Steelers beat the Broncos 33-10.

In 1979, Alzado went to Cleveland after a salary dispute. The Orange Crush was never the same.

Denver's Rick Upchurch slips past Kansas City defenders after catching a pass.

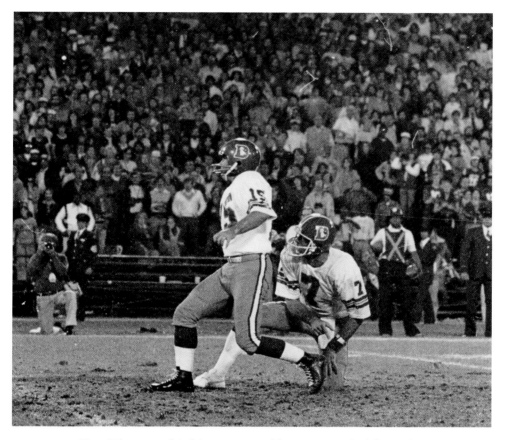

Jim Turner, kicking one of his many field goals.

On offense, Weese became the starting quarterback. But after six weeks, Morton replaced him. The Broncos remained tied for first place until December when the Seattle Seahawks defeated them 28-23. The Broncos made the playoffs as a wildcard team. But they did not go far, losing to Houston 13-7.

That same year, Denver kicker Jim Turner retired after 16 years in professional football. Turner converted 304 of 488 field goal attempts, making him one of pro football's all-time greatest kickers.

The Reeves Era

After the 1980 season, Red Miller left the Broncos. New owners hired Dan Reeves to replace Miller. Reeves was the NFL's youngest coach. But he had plenty of experience.

Reeves was a Dallas Cowboys running back from 1965 to 1972. From 1970 to 1980, Reeves was also one of the Cowboys coaches.

Reeves took over an old, injury-plagued team. He kept the defense together and named Morton the starting quarterback. By mid-November, the Broncos were in first place by one game. But then they lost to the Bengals and Chargers.

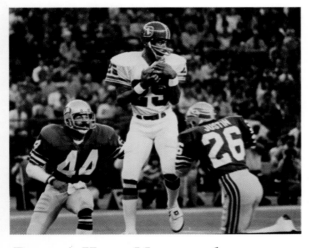

Denver's Haven Moses catches a pass between two Seahawks defenders.

Two wins put the Broncos one game ahead of the San Diego Chargers going into the final weekend. The Broncos played in Chicago and lost 35-24. When the Chargers beat Oakland on Monday night, San Diego won first place and the Broncos missed the playoffs.

In Reeves' second year, the Broncos collapsed. Bill Thompson retired. Steve Foley broke his arm on opening day and Bob Swenson held out for much of the season. Steve DeBerg replaced Morton at quarterback. The only bright spots were wide receivers Steve Watson and Rick Upchurch.

Elway Arrives

In 1983, the Denver Broncos signed rookie quarterback John Elway. Elway had huge potential, but he needed time to develop his skills. Reeves started Elway for the first five games, then replaced him with Steve DeBerg. DeBerg played the next five games, then suffered an injury. Elway returned and won three of six games—lifting the Broncos into the playoffs as a wildcard team against the Seattle Seahawks. Though Denver lost 31-7, Bronco fans knew Elway would only get better.

On September 9, 1984, Denver lost to Chicago 27-0. It was the Broncos only loss in their first 12 games. Elway was now the starting quarterback. He led the Broncos to a 13-3 record and the Western Division title. Even though Gradishar had retired and Swenson was injured, the defense also played well.

In his first playoff game, Elway could not solve the Pittsburgh defense. The Broncos lost 24-17 at Mile High Stadium. The Super Bowl would have to wait.

The following season, Denver set their sights on a championship. But two overtime losses to the Raiders within a three-week span late in the season kept the 11-5 Broncos out of the playoffs.

Tight end Lionel Taylor joins Denver in 1960.

Running back Otis Armstrong wins the rushing title in 1974.

Denver Broncos

Quarterback Frank Tripucka leads the Broncos to victory in 1960.

Tight end Riley Odoms becomes All-Pro in 1974.

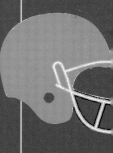

10   20   30   40

40

Lyle Alzado and the "Orange Crush" lead the Broncos to the Super Bowl in 1977.

2

Broncos coach Dan Reeves leads the Broncos to the AFC Western Conference championship in 1986.

Quarterback John Elway signs with Denver in 1983.

Linebacker Simon Fletcher leads the Broncos in sacks in 1993.

Denver Broncos

40   30   20   10

In 1986, Elway took control. He passed for 3,485 yards and led the Broncos to the divisional title. The Broncos started with a 6-0 record and finished 11-5.

In the playoffs, Elway won his first postseason game with a 22-17 victory over the New England Patriots. Elway's third-quarter, 48-yard pass to Vance Johnson put the Broncos in the lead. Jones' fourth-quarter safety finished the scoring. Now they would play the AFC championship game in frigid Cleveland against the Browns.

Broncos coach Dan Reeves is carried off the field by his players after winning the AFC Western Conference championship.

The Drive

Nearly 80,000 fans watched the Browns and Broncos battle to a 10-10 halftime tie. Rich Karlis kicked a 26-yard field goal for the only score in the third quarter. Early in the fourth quarter, Cleveland tied the game with a field goal. With less than six minutes remaining, Cleveland went ahead 20-13.

On the next kickoff, Gene Lang fumbled the ball before recovering at the Denver 2-yard line. The Broncos were 98 yards away from the tying touchdown.

Elway calmly led the Broncos on their longest drive of the game. With 1:48 remaining, he faced a 3rd-and-18 at the Cleveland 48. A 20-yard pass to Mark Jackson kept "The Drive" alive. Five plays later, Elway found Jackson in the endzone and sent the game into overtime.

Cleveland took the overtime kickoff but could not move the ball. Then Elway led the Broncos on another long drive. With 5:48 gone, Karlis lined up for a field goal at the Browns' 23-yard line. His kick curved left—but went through the uprights. The Broncos were AFC champions.

Denver faced the New York Giants in Super Bowl XXI. The Broncos took an early 10-9 lead, but then they collapsed. The Giants scored 17 points in the third quarter and went on to an impressive 39-20 victory. Elway passed for 304 yards, but the Broncos could not run the ball. Denver would have to wait for their first Super Bowl win.

Wide receiver Mark Jackson catches a 24-yard pass against the New York Giants in Super Bowl XXI.

Back-to-Back
Super Bowls

The next season, Elway was on top of his game. When the Broncos adopted the shotgun formation in their ninth game, Elway became even more dangerous. The formation gave him greater opportunity to scramble.

Elway often threw to the "Three Amigos"—wide receivers Vance Johnson, Mark Jackson, and Ricky Nattiel. On defense, Mecklenburg and Jones continued to play well. For the second straight year, the Broncos won their division. Once again, they faced the Cleveland Browns in the AFC championship game—this time, at Mile High Stadium.

In the first half, Elway led the Broncos to a 21-3 halftime lead. But Cleveland scored 21 third-quarter points and cut the lead to 31-24.

The Browns tied the game at 31-31 early in the fourth quarter. But Elway's 20-yard pass to Sammy Winder put Denver ahead again. Cleveland drove the field on their next series and threatened to tie the game once more. On second down at the Denver eight, Ernest Byner burst off tackle. But at the 2-yard line, Jeremiah Castille caused a fumble and the Broncos recovered. As the final seconds ticked away, Denver took a safety rather than punt from its own endzone, making the final score 38-33. For the second year in a row, the Broncos were in the Super Bowl.

At the start of the game, Elway hit Ricky Nattiel on a 56-yard scoring strike. Then Rich Karlis added a 24-yard field goal, making it 10-0 after the first quarter. But Denver would not score again. Washington exploded for 35 second-quarter points on its way to a 42-10 victory.

For the game, Elway completed only 14-of-38 attempts for 257 yards and three interceptions. Elway needed more help if Denver wanted to win an NFL championship.

In 1988, the Broncos signed former Cowboys running back Tony Dorsett, hoping he could improve their running game. But Elway's sore arm and injured receivers crippled the offense. Even worse, Mecklenburg suffered a hand injury. After the Broncos failed to make the playoffs, Reeves fired most of the defensive coaches, including coordinator Joe Collier, who had been with the Broncos for 20 years.

Elway about to attempt a pass against the Washington Redskins in Super Bowl XXII.

A Fourth Super Bowl

In 1989, Denver racked up the best record in the AFC and earned home field advantage throughout the playoffs. Reeves and new defensive coach Wade Phillips rebuilt the defense with cornerback Wymon Henderson, defensive end Alphonso Carreker, and top draft pick Steve Atwater. The defense allowed 126 fewer points than in 1988. Elway had an average season. But rookie running back Bobby Humphrey picked up the slack and rushed for over 1,000 yards.

In the first round of the playoffs, Denver beat Pittsburgh 24-23. Melvin Bratton won the game on a 1-yard run late in the fourth quarter.

In the AFC championship game, the Broncos and Browns met for the third time in four years. This time, it wasn't even close. Elway completed 20-of-36 passes for 385 yards and three touchdowns, and led his team in rushing. The Broncos blew the game open in the fourth quarter with 13 unanswered points as Denver won 37-21.

In the opening quarter of the Super Bowl, the San Francisco 49ers raced to a 13-3 lead. By halftime, it was 27-3. The game would only get worse.

San Francisco's 55-10 victory set many Super Bowl records, including the largest winning margin and the most points scored by one team. Meanwhile, Denver's fourth defeat tied the Minnesota Vikings for the most Super Bowl losses.

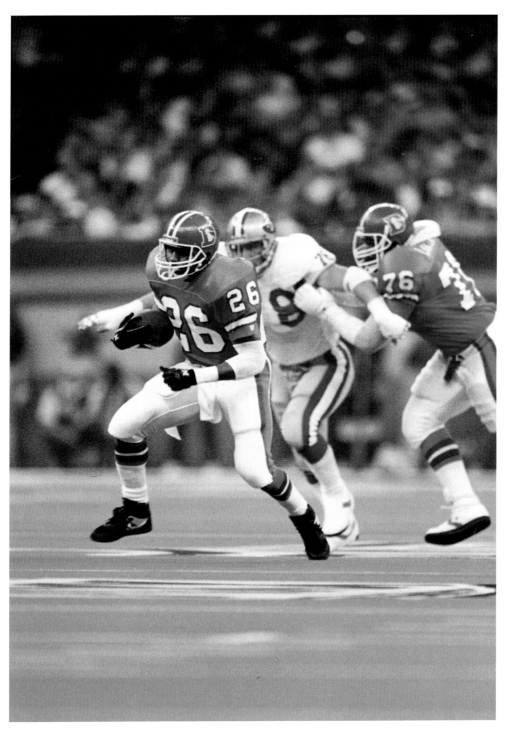

Rookie running back Bobby Humphrey rushed for 61 yards against the 49ers in Super Bowl XXIV.

The 1990s

The new decade did not start well for the Broncos. In 1990, Denver finished 5-11 as Elway had one of his poorest seasons. But the following year, the Broncos made the most dramatic improvement in team history, finishing 12-4 and wining the AFC West title. The Denver defense led the AFC in nearly every category, including fewest touchdowns allowed, fewest points allowed, most sacks, fewest third-down conversions, and fewest passing yards allowed. Newcomer Gaston Green turned into a 1,000-yard rusher.

Elway and Clarence Kay (88) try to regroup against the Bills in the AFC championship game.

In the playoffs, Denver trailed Houston 24-23 late in the fourth quarter. But then Elway led the Broncos on a long drive, setting up a 28-yard field goal by David Treadwell that won the game. The game-winning drive enhanced Elway's reputation for game-winning heroics. But Elway could not reproduce his magic in the AFC championship game against the Buffalo Bills as Denver lost 10-7.

In 1992, the Broncos started with a 7-3 mark. But Elway's injury spelled doom for the Broncos. He was replaced by Tommy Maddox and Shawn Moore, with little success. The Broncos were outscored by 67 points in their 16 games. Linebacker Simon Fletcher had a team-record 16 sacks, making it 10 or more for him in 4 consecutive seasons. After the 8-8 season, Dan Reeves was fired. Wade Phillips was promoted to head coach.

The coaching change seemed to revitalize John Elway. In 1993, Elway passed for a career-high 4,030 yards and 25 touchdowns. But the Broncos finished with a 9-7 record and a first-round playoff loss to the L.A. Raiders. Denver was the highest-scoring team in the conference, but the defense too often failed to hold onto leads and allowed too many big plays.

On the bright side, Shannon Sharpe had a great season with 81 catches for 995 yards and an AFC-best nine receiving touchdowns. Linebacker Simon Fletcher led the Broncos in sacks for the sixth straight season.

In 1994, the Broncos continued their slide from the top of the AFC. In the playoff hunt all season long, the Broncos finished with a 7-9 record. It was the last game for retiring linebacker Karl Mecklenburg. It also spelled doom for Wade Phillips, who finished his two-year stint as head coach with a 16-16 record.

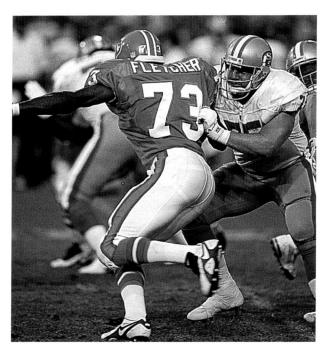

In 1993, linebacker Simon Fletcher led the Broncos in sacks for the sixth straight season.

A Super Bowl Ring
for Elway?

With a new coach and an aging team, the Broncos future seems uncertain. Though Elway remains one of the best quarterbacks in the NFL, his career is on the wane. But if management can surround him with talented offensive players and a strong defense, Elway still has the ability and experience to lead the Broncos to that elusive Super Bowl win.

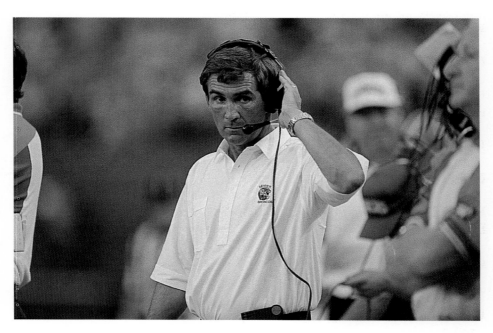

Head coach Mike Shanahan.

GLOSSARY

ALL-PRO—A player who is voted to the Pro Bowl.

BACKFIELD—Players whose position is behind the line of scrimmage.

CORNERBACK—Either of two defensive halfbacks stationed a short distance behind the linebackers and relatively near the sidelines.

DEFENSIVE END—A defensive player who plays on the end of the line and often next to the defensive tackle.

DEFENSIVE TACKLE—A defensive player who plays on the line and between the guard and end.

ELIGIBLE—A player who is qualified to be voted into the Hall of Fame.

END ZONE—The area on either end of a football field where players score touchdowns.

EXTRA POINT—The additional one-point score added after a player makes a touchdown. Teams earn an extra point if the placekicker kicks the ball through the uprights of the goalpost.

FIELD GOAL—A three-point score awarded when a placekicker kicks the ball through the uprights of the goalpost.

FULLBACK—An offensive player who often lines up farthest behind the front line.

FUMBLE—When a player loses control of the football.

GUARD—An offensive lineman who plays between the tackles and center.

GROUND GAME—The running game.

HALFBACK—An offensive player whose position is behind the line of scrimmage.

HALFTIME—The time period between the second and third quarters of a football game.

INTERCEPTION—When a defensive player catches a pass from an offensive player.

KICK RETURNER—An offensive player who returns kickoffs.

LINEBACKER—A defensive player whose position is behind the line of scrimmage.

LINEMAN—An offensive or defensive player who plays on the line of scrimmage.

PASS—To throw the ball.

PASS RECEIVER—An offensive player who runs pass routes and catches passes.

PLACEKICKER—An offensive player who kicks extra points and field goals. The placekicker also kicks the ball from a tee to the opponent after his team has scored.

PLAYOFFS—The postseason games played amongst the division winners and wild card teams which determines the Super Bowl champion.

PRO BOWL—The postseason All-Star game that showcases the NFL's best players.

PUNT—To kick the ball to the opponent.

QUARTER—One of four 15-minute time periods that makes up a football game.

QUARTERBACK—The backfield player who usually calls the signals for the plays.

REGULAR SEASON—The games played after the preseason and before the playoffs.

ROOKIE—A first-year player.

RUNNING BACK—A backfield player who usually runs with the ball.

RUSH—To run with the football.

SACK—To tackle the quarterback behind the line of scrimmage.

SAFETY—A defensive back who plays behind the linemen and linebackers. Also, two points awarded for tackling an offensive player in his own end zone when he's carrying the ball.

SPECIAL TEAMS—Squads of football players that perform special tasks (for example, kickoff team and punt-return team).

SPONSOR—A person or company that finances a football team.

SUPER BOWL—The NFL championship game played between the AFC champion and the NFC champion.

T FORMATION—An offensive formation in which the fullback lines up behind the center and quarterback with one halfback stationed on each side of the fullback.

TACKLE—An offensive or defensive lineman who plays between the ends and the guards.

TAILBACK—The offensive back farthest from the line of scrimmage.

TIGHT END—An offensive lineman who is stationed next to the tackles, and who usually blocks or catches passes.

TOUCHDOWN—When one team crosses the goal line of the other team's end zone. A touchdown is worth six points.

TURNOVER—To turn the ball over to an opponent either by a fumble, an interception, or on downs.

TWO-POINT CONVERSION—The additional two points scored after a player makes a touchdown. Teams earn the extra two points if an offensive player crosses the goal line with the football before being tackled.

UNDERDOG—The team that is picked to lose the game.

WIDE RECEIVER—An offensive player who is stationed relatively close to the sidelines and who usually catches passes.

WILD CARD—A team that makes the playoffs without winning its division.

ZONE PASS DEFENSE—A pass defense method where defensive backs defend a certain area of the playing field rather than individual pass receivers.

INDEX